THE AWFUL APPLE ORCHARD

M. D. Spenser

Plantation, Florida

Published by Paradise Press, Inc. by arrangement with River Publishing, Inc. All right, title and interest to the "SHIVERS" logo and design are owned by River Publishing, Inc. No portion of the "SHIVERS" logo and design may be reproduced in part or whole without prior written permission from River Publishing, Inc. An application for a registered trademark of the "SHIVERS" logo and design is pending with the Federal Patent and Trademark office.

ISBN 1-57657-047-9

EXCLUSIVE DISTRIBUTION BY PARADISE PRESS, INC.

Cover Design by George Paturzo

Cover Illustration by Eddie Roseboom

Printed in the U.S.A.

30585

DO YOU ENJOY BEING FRIGHTENED?

WOULD YOU RATHER HAVE
NIGHTMARES
INSTEAD OF SWEET DREAMS?

ARE YOU HAPPY ONLY WHEN
SHAKING WITH FEAR?

CONGRATULATIONS ! ! ! !

YOU'VE MADE A WISE CHOICE.

THIS BOOK IS THE DOORWAY
TO ALL THAT MAY FRIGHTEN YOU.

GET READY FOR

COLD, CLAMMY SHIVERS
RUNNING UP AND DOWN YOUR SPINE!

NOW, OPEN THE DOOR—
IF YOU DARE !!!!

To Bob, Mary, Daniel, and Sara

Chapter One

"This is going to be the best vacation we ever had!" Sara said again. She had been saying it about every fifteen minutes since we had gotten into the car.

Usually, that sort of thing drives me nuts. A year of age makes a huge difference in people's maturity. I'm twelve. Sara is eleven.

But this time I just kept my mouth shut. After all, it was my fault that we had not taken this vacation in the summer, and that we almost missed it entirely.

Of course, it was also my "fault," if you want to put it that way, that Sara and I were excused from two weeks of school to take this family vacation in October.

But I figured if I said anything to her now, she would remind everybody that we'd almost had no vacation at all because of me. So I just kept quiet.

"You know, Sara," Mom said over her shoulder from the front seat, “I think you’re right.”

And then she said, “Oh!” and turned to face Dad, who was driving.

“Bob, I just remembered the mill. Let’s stop there on the way to the cabin and get some apples and cider.”

“Sure,” Dad said. “It’s on the way.”

“What kind of a mill?” I asked.

“It’s a very old cider mill,” Mom said, “and they make great apple cider. They have their own orchard, so they even grow their own apples. And you can go inside the mill and actually watch the apples being crushed and the cider being made.”

“Oh,” Sara said.

“Cool,” I said.

“And besides,” Dad said, without taking his eyes off the road, “there’s even some old story about the mill and the orchard being haunted. Your mother and I heard that when we were there a few years ago.”

“Haunted?” Sara said. She did not exactly sound thrilled.

“That makes it extra cool!” I said.

But when I really started to think about it, a

cold, clammy shiver came over me. I wasn't sure why. Even though I knew — or *thought* I knew — that there were no such things as haunted buildings, I was siezed by a sense of foreboding and dread.

Chapter Two

In the car, Sara just gave me a dirty look and went back to watching the countryside roll by. Every mile of the New York State Thruway fascinated her.

We rode in silence for a few minutes, and then Sara called out again.

"Look! Over there! Cows! There's a whole herd of cows!"

"Sara," I said, "there are four cows, not a herd."

I couldn't help it.

"I like cows!" Sara said.

"Daniel, let your sister enjoy the cows," Dad said. "Besides, once we get to the cabin, you're going to see about a million times more apples than cows. New York State is famous for its apples."

"And its haunted cider mills!" I said, looking at Sara.

She just shot me another dirty look without saying anything.

Mom said, "You know, that mill is close enough for you two to ride your bikes there. You could take a ride there every day and we could have fresh cider every day."

"Sure, Mom," I said. "I'm glad we brought them."

It had been my idea to bring the bikes, and they were riding now on the top of the car.

A few minutes later, Dad said, "Here we go," and steered the car into the exit lane.

We all cheered.

After paying the toll, Dad turned the car onto a narrow country road that twisted and turned constantly. Along the sides of the road were some small patches of woods and a lot of farmers' fields and really old, red barns.

"We're getting close," Dad said.

It was the middle of October, so all the leaves on the trees along the road had turned yellow and gold and red. They were just beginning to drop off the branches, and a few brightly colored leaves littered the road and the edges of the fields.

"You know what I'm going to do?" Sara said to no one in particular.

"You're going to collect leaves," I said right away.

"That's right," Sara said, speaking with dignity. "And they're going to be the most beautiful leaves in the world."

"Bob, remember to stop for cider," Mom said to Dad.

I have to admit that I was sitting forward on the seat, looking out the window just like Sara, now that we were getting so close to the cabin.

And to the "haunted" cider mill.

Before I even knew what I was doing, I was shouting myself.

"Hey, look at the horses!"

"Well," Sara said smugly, "look who's shouting about animals now."

Then Dad said, "Here's the turn for the cider mill."

We turned onto a gravel road beside a house that looked as if it might fall down at any minute. The road was bumpy and Dad had to let the car just crawl along slowly.

"There it is," Mom said.

The cider mill was a big red building, sort of like a barn. There were lots of cars parked in a field beside it, and lots of people going in and out.

"That doesn't look haunted," Sara said.

"Well, you never know," Dad said.

He brought the car to a stop at the side of the road. "This place is about a hundred years old. You never know what might have happened here during all those years."

"You bet," I said, hoping to make Sara more frightened. "The places that are haunted worst are the ones that don't look like they're haunted at all."

"Knock it off, Daniel," Sara said. "I know you're just trying to scare me."

I could see she was looking nervous, and I was going to say something else when Mom spoke up.

"I'll just run in and get cider for today. You kids can explore and see if it's haunted another time."

"Sure, Mom," I said. "Right, Sara? We'll come back tomorrow on our bikes and see if it's haunted."

"Sure," Sara said. She was making her face look very brave. "I'm not the least little bit afraid. And, besides, I don't care if it *is* haunted. This is going to be the best vacation we ever had."

Chapter Three

This was a vacation that almost did not happen.

And, like so many things in my world, it was my fault.

We had been planning this trip to the cabin in the Catskills since the spring. It was going to be great for everybody.

Dad said he would like to go book-hunting in some of the "book barns" upstate.

Mom said she would like the loneliness and the quiet. She just wanted to sit in the sunshine and maybe take some long walks. And she did not want to do any driving.

Sara was looking forward to the beautiful scenery and the fall colors and the farms. She was going to bring her pencils and drawing pads.

I wanted to explore the lonely country roads on my bike, and I was also hoping Dad would take me horseback riding.

I was the one who suggested that Sara and I should bring our bikes.

"And not be asking Mom to drive all the time," Mom said.

That clinched it. Dad called the owners that same evening and reserved the cabin for the first two weeks in July.

And then, on June 29, I nearly got killed riding my bike.

It had been raining all day. When it stopped in the afternoon, I got my bike out of the garage and got on it and started fast down our driveway.

I made a sharp left onto the sidewalk. But I was going too fast. The tires slipped on the wet driveway. The bike slid out from under me and crashed into the fire hydrant at the curb near the end of the driveway.

And me?

I went sailing through the air like I'd been shot out of a cannon. I landed in a heap in the middle of the wet road. For a few seconds, I didn't even know what happened. But I did hear the brakes of a car screeching to a halt. It stopped just a second before it would have run me over.

My bike was fine. It did not even have a scratch on it.

But I was a wreck!

I scraped one of my knees so badly that it was bleeding. I twisted my other ankle so much that I couldn't walk on it for more than a week. And I hit my head so hard I had a headache for days.

Once my parents stopped thinking I was going to die, you can bet they laid into me pretty hard about riding my bike carelessly.

And then, of course, the worst part was that we could not go on our vacation in July.

And, naturally, it was all my fault.

You can imagine how happy I was a couple of months later when Mom and Dad said we were going to the cabin for two weeks in October.

That also meant that Sara and I would miss two weeks of school. Mom went to school and talked to the principal. The principal was not too pleased, I guess.

But Sara and I both had excellent grades. We just had to promise that we would catch up on everything we missed.

That was a promise that was easy to make in return for two weeks off.

I was glad we were going on vacation. I was glad we were missing school for two weeks. And I was almost glad I'd had that accident on the bike.

But if I had known what was going to happen at that old cider mill, I would have been glad to just stay at home and go to school.

At least the school doesn't have ghosts that try to kill people.

Chapter Four

While Mom went inside the mill to get cider, I checked the place out from the car.

It really did look very ordinary. There were doors at the front where you could go in to buy cider and apples. It looked like they had other stuff for sale, too, like apple pies and donuts. Most of the people were going in there.

At the side of the place, a kind of rickety stairway went up to the second floor. A sign on the wall said: "SEE THE MILL AT WORK!"

Off to the side, a little building with a window and counter sold hot dogs and hamburgers and donuts and paper cups of cider.

And behind the mill, I could just see a little bit of the apple orchard.

Everything looked normal. The trees grew in

neat rows and stretched back as far as I could see. Under the trees, between the straight rows, a small tractor was pulling a wagon loaded with red apples.

Nothing looked spooky or creepy or scary. But, of course, that could be the creepiest thing of all.

A shiver ran up my spine.

Then Mom was back at the car with a plastic jug of cider. Dad started the car and we went forward, past the front of the mill.

We came to another road and Dad turned the car to the right.

This gave me a good view of the side and back of the mill, and also a good view of the apple orchard.

I was looking closely at it, with my face against the glass of the window.

Suddenly, I became aware of Sara leaning over against me. She was looking out at the orchard, too.

I glanced at her over my shoulder. Our eyes met.

I knew we were both thinking the same thing.

This time my nerve failed me and I said nothing.

I turned away from Sara and looked back

again at the orchard. The road was just curving away from it. I told myself that I was being silly.

Of course, the mill wasn't haunted.

Of course, the orchard wasn't haunted.

Those things just don't happen in real life.

That's when something very hard hit the window I was looking out!

"What was that?" Dad said.

When the thing hit the window, I jumped back in the seat. I crashed into Sara. I looked at her for a second. Her face was as white as a sheet.

"I . . . I don't know, Dad," I said. I was so shaken up, I could hardly talk.

The car wasn't going fast but Dad slowed down even more. He glanced over his shoulder at the right rear window, the one right beside my head.

I was so frightened I couldn't think straight. But Dad saw the wet smear on the window and knew at once what had hit us.

"An apple," he said. "Somebody threw an apple at the car."

Sure enough, that's exactly what it was. It had splattered all over the window. There was clear apple juice on the glass. Little bits of crushed apple pulp had slid down to the bottom of the window.

I swung around on the back seat.

We were passing a big empty field on the right side of the road. And I could see the road for a long distance behind us.

The road and the field were both empty.

I felt Sara's hand clutching at my arm.

There was nobody there!

Chapter Five

The cabin was really hidden away, in among the hills and farms and woods.

While Dad drove, I made an effort to remember the roads and each place where he turned.

But this was not like the city or the suburbs. These roads had no names or numbers. You just had to remember them.

When we reached the cabin, Dad just wiped the crushed apple off the car window and muttered about how there were "bad kids" even out here in the country.

Sara and I looked at each other, but neither one of us said a word.

We didn't have a chance to talk until later that evening.

The cabin had a bedroom for Mom and Dad,

and another, smaller room with two bunk beds. We could each have a top bunk.

Once we were in there and the lights were out, I whispered across to Sara.

"Do you want to go to the mill tomorrow?"

"I don't know," she whispered back. "Do you?"

"I guess so. Anyway, Mom will want us to go."

"Yeah."

"Yeah."

For a minute, all the things we weren't saying just hung there in the darkness.

"So I guess we'll go to the mill tomorrow," I whispered.

"I guess."

"It'll be okay."

I heard Sara sigh in the darkness. "I guess," she whispered.

Then I said what I was really thinking.

"That apple," I said. "There was nobody around who could have thrown it."

"Maybe we just didn't look hard enough,"

Sara whispered.

I did not answer her. I just thought about that empty field and that empty road and that apple hitting the car.

After a few seconds, Sara whispered, "Yeah, you're right. There was nobody there."

I heard her take a deep breath. I could tell from the way it sounded that she was shivering.

I took a deep breath myself. Most of the time, Sara annoys me and I just like to tease her. But sometimes it feels good to be a real big brother to her. Anyway, I had to look out for her, no matter what. She was my little sister. I just had to.

I whispered across the darkness to her.

"Don't worry. That place probably isn't haunted, anyway. And even if it is, I'll protect you."

Usually, Sara would make some smart-aleck remark to something like that. This time, her voice sounded very, very tiny in the darkness.

"Thank you," she whispered, so softly that I could barely hear her.

Oh, boy, I thought. This time, I'm going to have my hands full.

Chapter Six

"Are you two going to ride your bikes to the mill today?" Mom asked.

We were finishing breakfast. With the sun shining in the windows, and all the bright fall colors on the trees outside, I had forgotten all about the mill.

"Uh, yeah, I guess so," I said.

Sara got really busy with the rest of her scrambled eggs.

Mom was not really trying to get rid of us. It just felt that way because I was in no hurry to go.

But in about a minute — that's the way it felt — Sara and I were outside, sitting on our bikes.

I had four five-dollar bills in my pocket. I also had a piece of paper with a map to the mill that Dad had drawn on it. And I had another piece of paper that reminded me to get half a gallon of cider and a peck of

McIntosh apples.

"Gee, Mom," I started to say. "I'm not sure I can ride and . . ."

That's when Dad appeared from inside with something shiny in his hand.

"Look, Daniel," he said. "Here's a basket for your bike."

Oh, great! I was going to look like a total nerd with a basket on my bike. I probably had the only basket for two hundred miles around.

I think it took Dad exactly twelve seconds to attach the basket to my handlebars.

"There you go," he said. He was very pleased with the quick job he'd done.

"Great, Dad," I said weakly. "Thanks."

"Daniel," my mother said, "with that basket, maybe you could get a nice apple pie, too. You have enough money."

"Okay," I said. I was starting to feel like a condemned man going to face the firing squad.

"C'mon, Sara," I said.

We started down the hill from our cabin to the nearest road.

"Be careful around cars!" Mom called after us.

"And keep an eye out for ghosts!" Dad yelled. "You know, that place might really be haunted!"

Oh, great, I thought. What was going on here? Was this some sort of terrible trap Sara and I had fallen into?

Then I remembered the other piece of paper in the pocket of my jeans. Mom had written the name of the farm our cabin was on and the telephone number of the nearest farmhouse.

Terrific, I thought to myself.

Now when the ghost got through with us, whoever found us would know where to bring what was left.

If there was anything left at all.

Chapter Seven

The mill was much farther away than it had seemed in the car. It took us about half an hour to get there on our bikes.

And we were bushed when we arrived. There were so many hills and mountains in that part of the country that, at least half the time, we were riding or pushing our bikes uphill.

We were both thirsty when we got there.

"Let's get some cold cider first," I said to Sara.

"Okay," she said. "And donuts."

I looked over to where the cider and donuts were sold. "Fresh Baked," the sign said.

I began to think maybe we had both been a little silly. After all, the only thing we knew was that Dad had said the mill *might* be haunted. It wasn't a fact.

"Maybe Dad was just having some fun with us," I said.

"Yeah," Sara said. "Maybe that's it."

We got our cider and donuts and carried them to a bench behind the mill. I had seen some benches there, right beside a little pond.

The cider was cold and the donuts were the most delicious donuts I'd ever tasted.

We sat there, drinking the cold cider and munching on donuts. I began to think that I must have been crazy to believe a place like this could be haunted.

We looked around at all the people coming and going, laughing and talking, drinking cider and eating donuts just like us.

Lots of people were buying apples and cider and bringing them back to their cars.

The sun was shining and a cool breeze was blowing.

Yep, I thought, I must have been nuts to think a place like this could be haunted.

"I want another donut," I said to Sara. "You

want one?"

"Yep," she said.

"Okay," I said, "I'll get them. You wait here."

I headed around to the side of the mill and the separate little building where they sold food. There were four people ahead of me on line, so I had to wait a few minutes until it was my turn.

But that turned out to be lucky, because a whole new batch of donuts was brought out just as I got up to the counter.

Those donuts smelled so good it almost made me dizzy. My mouth was watering, just thinking about them.

I paid my money, took the donuts wrapped up in paper napkins, and started back toward the little pond behind the mill.

I could smell those donuts and feel how warm they were through the napkins.

I came around the back corner of the mill, heading toward our bench.

I stopped short.

The bench was empty.

Sara was gone!

Chapter Eight

"Sara!" I yelled.

I spun around. My eyes swept across the pond. Was she in there? Was she drowning? Where was she?

In half a second, I looked everywhere. I couldn't see her!

"Daniel! I'm up here."

My head snapped up. There she was.

The rickety-looking stairway at the side of the mill went up to a platform just around the back, where a door led inside.

Sara was up there on the platform, looking down at me.

"Come up," she called. "Wait'll you see what's up here!"

You wait, I thought to myself, and see what I do when I get my hands on you!

I raced around to the side of the mill and up that narrow, shaky staircase to the platform. As I came around the corner, Sara disappeared through the doorway.

I dove after her just as the door closed in my face.

I went to grab the doorknob and that's when I realized I still had the donuts in my hands. I had to switch one of them into the other hand before I could open the door.

Sara was smart. She knew I wouldn't yell at her in front of other people.

And there were a dozen or more people in there. It was a gift shop, and it was packed with stuff.

There were little scarecrows and painted wooden apples and plates and dishes with pictures of the mill on them, and little rocking horses, and all sorts of things.

But where was Sara?

I hurried down the first aisle and caught sight of her going through a doorway at the end of the room. I had to push past some people blocking the aisle in order to catch up with her.

"Look in here!" Sara whispered to me before I could even open my mouth.

The room was filled with the strong smell of fresh, sweet apples. It was a good smell, but it was so strong that it almost made me dizzy.

Actually, the room was really a sort of balcony. There was a little fence right in front of us.

On the other side of the fence was a huge piece of machinery. A gigantic turntable was moving slowly. Big wooden baskets were on it. Above it I could see apples rolling down a wooden chute into a kind of box above the baskets.

And someplace deep inside, where we could not see what was going on, the machinery was making a horrible, wet, chomping sound. To me, it sounded exactly like the noise a monster would make while it was chewing up the flesh and bones of a person.

Globbeta-glotch! Globbeta-glotch! Globbeta-glotch! Globbeta-glotch!

Suddenly, I noticed the floor shivering beneath my feet. It was shaking in time with the sound of the horrible machinery.

Globbeta-glotch! Globbeta-glotch! Globbeta-

glotch! Globbeta-glotch!

"Isn't this interesting?" I heard a man beside me say to his family.

"Yeah, Dad," two of his kids said together. "I never saw anything like this."

Well, I had never seen anything like this, either. But I had already seen enough to last me a good long time.

The floor beneath my feet was still shaking and quaking along with the horrible noise.

Globbeta-glotch! Globbeta-glotch! Globbeta-glotch! Globbeta-glotch!

"That's it!" I said.

I grabbed Sara's arm.

"We're outta here!"

I don't know how I did it, but in about a quarter of a second, Sara and I were across the gift shop, down the aisle, out the door, down the stairs, and back in the bright sunshine outside.

"You know, Daniel," Sara said, "sometimes you act like such a jerk!"

I stared at her in disbelief.

"Oh, good," she said. "You got the donuts. I

hope they're still warm. I like them best when they're warm."

I didn't even know I still had the donuts in my hand. They were almost crushed, I was holding them so tight.

At that moment, I did not care that she was my sister. And if the machinery inside the mill wanted to grab her up and gulp her down and go *globbeta-glotch!* on her flesh and bones, that was just fine with me.

Chapter Nine

Then, in about two seconds more, I felt like a complete idiot.

I had made a fool of myself again.

Running away because I was frightened by the sound of the machinery! It was just the mill grinding apples to make cider.

What was wrong with me?

I took some deep breaths to calm myself down.

Sara was eating her donut and looking around, as if nothing unusual had happened.

Maybe she knew I felt stupid and, for once, decided not to say anything to make me feel worse.

I waited a few seconds more to make sure my voice would be steady before I spoke. And then I said just one thing.

"Don't ever disappear like that again!"

Sara avoided meeting my eyes.

"I won't," she said.

And before I could say anything else, she added, "I promise."

I wasn't looking too good just then, so I thought I should just change the subject.

"When we finish these donuts, we better just get that stuff for Mom," I said.

"Okay."

By now, I really thought I must have gone nuts inside there. What was wrong with me? I never get really scared like that, for no good reason at all. Never!

Well, hardly ever.

We headed around to the front of the mill and went inside. There was a long line of people ahead of us and it took several minutes before we got our stuff.

I paid for it and counted my change. I'd had enough trouble already today. I didn't want to feel foolish again.

Anyway, now we could go. We had the bag of apples and the half-gallon of cider and the apple pie.

But then Sara decided she was still hungry.

Sometimes I just cannot believe how much food that child eats.

"Let's have an apple before we go," she said.

I sighed. Obviously, it was going to be one of those days when nothing goes right and I can't do a thing about it.

We strolled back to the bench beside the pond, where we had been sitting before.

I put the apples and the cider on the bench between us and Sara put down the pie. She pulled an apple out of the sack and took a big bite. I didn't feel like eating anything else right then.

"C'mon, Sara," I said. "Hurry up with that apple. We have a long ride back to the cabin."

Sara didn't say anything. She just stared down at the apple she'd taken a bite from.

I could see how wide open and horrified her eyes looked.

Then she started to scream.

Chapter Ten

"What's the matter?" I yelled. "What happened?"

It was as if she could not even hear me. She just kept staring at the apple in her hand.

All around us, out of the corners of my eyes, I could see people turning to stare at us.

"Sara!" I said. "What's the matter?"

"Look!" she said. Her voice sounded as if she were choking.

I looked at the apple in her hand. I could see the spot where she had taken a big bite from it.

And then I saw something else.

There was a hole in the red skin of the apple, right beside the line where her teeth had sunk into the fruit. And something was sticking up out of the apple.

And it was moving.

It was a worm!

And it was alive!

Sara made some horrible, strangled noise in her throat. She was trembling all over. And she was staring in horror at the worm.

"Yuck!" she said.

Then she started saying it like she was never going to stop.

"Yuck! Yuck! Yuck! Yuck! Yuck! Yuck!"

She still had the apple in her hand.

"Put it down," I said.

Sara dropped the apple as if it were a hand grenade that was about to explode.

Behind us, I heard somebody laugh.

"Find a worm?" somebody said, and I heard other voices laughing.

I choked back what I really wanted to say to those people.

"Daniel," I heard Sara say in her tiniest little voice.

I looked back at her.

"Let's just go back to the cabin. Right away. Okay? Okay?"

I thought she was going to burst out crying.

"Right!" I said. "Let's get going."

Sara was up off the bench like a shot. Somehow, she managed to pick up the bag of apples, the plastic jug of cider, and the apple pie. She was not wasting any time.

In a second, she was hurrying off toward where we had left our bikes.

I stood still for a second and looked down at the apple. It was lying right there on the grass in front of the bench, where Sara had dropped it.

Something looked strange about it.

I moved it a little with the toe of my sneaker.

I could see the spot where Sara had taken a bite. And I could see all the bright red skin that surrounded the spot she had bitten.

The red skin was perfect.

There was no hole in it anywhere.

And there was certainly no worm.

Chapter Eleven

That was a long ride back to the cabin.

For about fifteen minutes, we didn't even talk.

Finally, I had to tell Sara what I'd seen. Or, rather, what I had not seen.

"Sara, I have to tell you something," I said. "I looked at that apple after you dropped it. I looked really closely at it. There was no worm in it."

"What do you mean, there was no worm in it?" Sara said. "Of course, there was a worm in it, stupid. I saw it. I almost bit into it. It was gross! Yuck!"

I hardly knew how to say what I needed to tell her.

"Sara, I know you saw a worm in the apple. I saw it, too. I know it was there when you took a bite. Or, at least, it was there right after you took a bite."

"It was there!" Sara said.

"I know, I know," I said quickly.

"It was!" Sara said.

"Yes, it was. But, as soon as you dropped the apple, the worm just . . . well, the worm just disappeared."

Sara stopped her bike and turned and stared at me.

"Disappeared? The worm disappeared?"

"Yes."

"No!"

How long was she going to keep this up?

"The worm disappeared," I said firmly.

Sara thought about that for a few seconds. Then a deep frown creased her forehead.

"That means . . ." she said.

I had already figured out what it meant, but I waited to let Sara figure it out for herself.

"That means," she began again, speaking very slowly, "that if we had shown the apple to anybody else, they wouldn't have seen the worm."

"Right," I said softly. That was exactly what it meant.

"Oh, no," Sara said softly.

"Oh, yes," I said.

"So anybody who we told about it or showed it to . . ."

"Go on," I said.

Now a look of real horror came over Sara's face.

"They would have thought we were crazy!"

"Exactly," I said.

"So everybody will tell us there's nothing there," she said.

"Right."

"And nobody will help us," she said. Her voice was starting to shake now.

"Right," I said.

"Well, that's it!" Sara said. "That's it! I'm never going back to that cider mill, not even for a million dollars!"

"That's the worst part," I said. "We are going back. We'll have to."

"I'm not!"

"You are," I told her. "For a simple reason. Tomorrow, Mom will want us to go back for . . ."

"Then you go!" Sara shouted.

"She'll expect both of us to go."

"You go alone!" Sara insisted.

"Listen to me," I said. "Mom will expect us to go together. So we have to leave the cabin together."

"I'll wait someplace for you," Sara said. But I think she was beginning to see that she was trapped.

I tried to sound grown-up and serious when I spoke again.

"Just listen," I said carefully. "You can't wait for me someplace — for two reasons. First, you'll be afraid to wait by yourself. And second, I'm not going to let you out of my sight."

Sara looked as if she wanted to cry and scream and punch somebody, all at the same time.

"But the ghost — or the thing, or whatever it is — can't get us when we're far away from the mill, right?" she asked.

I thought about that.

"I don't think so," I said. "But we can't be sure about it, so we'll just have to wait and see."

Sara groaned.

Before we got back on our bikes, we checked the road behind us. We didn't see anything. We checked the woods on one side of the road and the field on the other, but we didn't see anything there, either.

But that didn't mean there was nothing there.

We rode the rest of the way back to the cabin in silence. I kept thinking about the question Sara had asked.

Could the thing at the cider mill — if there *was* a thing at the cider mill — get to us and hurt us anyplace else? Like on this road? Or at the cabin?

I did not have to wait long to find out.

When we reached the cabin and pushed our bikes up the last part of the slope, Mom was sitting on the porch.

"Did you kids have a good time?" she asked.

"Sure, Mom," we said together.

"Here, I'll take those things inside."

She took the apples and the cider and the pie out of the basket Dad had attached to my handlebars.

I'd had so much on my mind, I hadn't even thought about that stupid basket for hours.

"You two put your bikes around back, where the car is. Then come inside for your lunch."

We walked the bikes along the side of the cabin. I was going first. I was just about to lean my bike against the cabin wall when I saw something I could hardly believe.

I stopped short.

Sara rolled the front wheel of her bike against the back of my legs.

"Oh, no!" I groaned. "Oh, no!"

"What?" I heard Sara say behind me.

All I could say was, "Oh, no!"

"What?" Sara cried out. "Daniel, what's the matter?"

Chapter Twelve

"Look!" I said.

I pointed at the car.

"Look!" I said again.

Sara leaned her bike against the cabin wall behind mine. Together, we edged forward, closer to the car.

All the doors of the car were closed and all the windows were rolled up. The car looked normal in every way.

Except for one thing.

It was filled, right up to the roof, with apples!

"Oh, no!" Sara whispered. "What are we going to do?"

I was trying to think fast.

"Nothing," I said. "Nothing. Not right now."

I had to stop to take a deep breath.

"We'll just go inside and eat lunch like nothing happened," I said.

"I can't eat!" Sara said.

"Oh, yes, you can," I told her.

"No, I can't!" Sara said. "And I'm frightened, and I'm going to tell Dad!"

I grabbed her arm.

"No, you're not!" I said. I had to struggle to keep my voice down. "Remember the worm!" I said.

Sara's hands flew up to her face.

"I forgot!" she cried. "He won't be able to see them."

"Right," I said.

I looked back at the car. It was still filled with apples. I could hardly believe my eyes.

"Okay," I said. "Here's my plan. We're going to go inside and eat lunch. And we'll act like nothing has happened. Then we just have to hope and hope that Dad doesn't want to drive anyplace."

Sara had her eyes closed, she was hoping so hard.

"Then, after lunch," I said, "we'll come out here and empty the car. We'll just have to toss the apples into the woods behind the cabin."

But suddenly Sara had an idea.

"Wait a minute," she said. "If we're the only ones who can see the apples, then Mom and Dad can't."

"Well . . ." I said. I had to think about that for a second.

"Maybe," I said. "But we can't be sure. They might be able to feel them or something. Or smell them. And they'd think we put them there."

Sara started to say something, but I stopped her and continued talking.

"Or they might see and feel and smell nothing," I said. "And we won't be able to get into the car when they want to go someplace. And they won't believe us if we tell them why. No, the only thing we can do is empty the car ourselves."

Sara's chin dropped to her chest. She looked totally defeated.

"I guess so," she said in that little voice.

"C'mon," I said.

We headed toward the door at the front of the cabin.

"Just act normal," I whispered.

"Okay," she whispered back.

I wasn't sure she was going to be able to act normal.

And then, when I opened the door and stepped inside the cabin, I wasn't sure if I would be able to act normal myself.

I was staring at the table Mom had set for lunch.

"Hi," said Dad. He was just sitting down at the table.

"Hi," I said. But I wasn't looking at him.

I was staring at the table.

Behind me, Sara bumped into me in the doorway.

"Hurry up and wash your hands," Mom said. "I made peanut butter and jelly sandwiches for you. And there's a big cold glass of apple cider waiting right there for each of you."

"Thanks, Mom," I managed to say. But it sounded just like a croak.

I'm sure that when Mom and Dad looked at the table, they saw glasses of normal apple cider. And the glasses next to Mom's plate and Dad's plate sure looked like ordinary glasses of cider.

But the glasses next to the other two plates, Sara's and mine, looked exactly like big, tall, glasses of blood!

"Daniel," I heard Mom saying. "What's the matter? You look like you've just seen a ghost!"

"Say," Dad said. "That reminds me."

He looked at Sara and me and winked.

"You guys didn't see any ghosts around that mill, did you?"

All I could do was stare at him.

"You know," he said, "the ghosts that are supposed to haunt the place are kids about your ages. It's a sad story. About a hundred years ago, these two kids were playing in the mill and they got caught in the machinery."

"Oh, Bob!" Mom said. "That's a horrible story!"

"Well," Dad said, "that's the story, anyhow." He looked at Sara and me again. "You guys didn't see any ghosts, right?"

Chapter Thirteen

It was not easy getting through that meal.

I had to force myself to eat. That peanut butter just stuck inside my mouth. I still don't know how I ever managed to swallow any of it.

Sara hardly ate anything at all.

I kept staring at that glass of blood, right there beside my plate.

I saw Sara was staring at hers, too, with her eyes wide open in horror. I kicked her twice under the table but she didn't even look at me either time.

And every two seconds — at least, that's what it seemed like — Mom kept urging us to drink our apple juice. I nearly gagged every time I looked at that glass.

And, besides telling us to drink the juice, Mom kept saying there was apple pie for dessert.

Sara just put her head down to hide her face. And she kept it down.

Finally, I had to say something.

"Uh, Mom," I began. I didn't even know what I was going to say.

"Yes, Daniel?"

My mind was racing.

"Well, Mom," I began again, "I think maybe we already had too many apples today."

"Too many?" Mom said. "What do you mean? Did you have some apples while you were at the mill?"

That's when Sara decided to put in her two cents' worth.

"Yeah, that's it, Mom," she said. "Right. We ate too many apples while we were at the mill."

Mom looked as if she did not believe a word of it.

Dad was eating a ham and cheese sandwich. Now he put it down on his plate. He looked first at Sara and then at me.

"Exactly what is going on here?" he said. He used that really tired voice he uses when he's not really very upset.

I was afraid Sara was going to blow the whole thing. I spoke up quickly.

"Well, see," I said, "we had some donuts and then some cider and then some apples and . . ."

"And now you're full, right?" Dad said.

"Right!" I said. "We just ate too much."

Dad stood up.

"Well, I don't know about you," he said, "but I'm on vacation. And I'm going inside to take a nap."

He stopped and turned back to Mom.

"Mary," he said to her, "what are the chances of having some baked apples?"

Mom smiled at him.

"The chances are excellent," she said. "We all love baked apples. I'll do some later."

"Thanks," Dad said. Then he looked at Sara and me.

"And I hope you two will try to keep the noise down to a dull roar, okay?"

"Sure, Dad," I said.

He headed for the bedroom.

Please, oh, please, don't look out the window, I kept thinking over and over.

I didn't breathe again until I heard the bed creak in the other room.

But Mom still looked as if she knew something was wrong. We had to get out of there.

I sat back in my chair and patted my stomach.

"Wow, I'm full," I said. "Guess I ate too much today."

Sara took the hint.

"Yeah, me too," she said. "I'm really full."

Mom sighed. "I don't know what's going on here," she said. "But I think you two need to get a lot more fresh air."

She shook her head to show that she was annoyed, but only a little.

"Go ahead," she said. "I'll clean up."

"Thanks, Mom," we said together.

We were out of there in about a second.

The instant we were outside the door, we raced around the corner of the cabin and down to the back, where the car was.

This time, it was Sara who stopped short and cried out, "Oh, no!"

I crashed right into her.

"Oh, no!" I said.

All the apples that had been inside the car were gone.

But the car was gone, too!

Chapter Fourteen

Sara had her hands up to her cheeks.

She just kept whispering the same thing over and over and over.

"Oh, no! Oh, no! Oh, no! Oh, no! Oh, no!"

I was not doing much better.

I could not think straight. My mind just kept racing.

This was the worst thing that had happened. The car was gone!

But it was even worse than that.

If the ghost or whatever it was could make a whole car disappear, what else could it do?

"Stay calm," I told Sara. "Just stay calm!"

That was a stupid thing to say, because I certainly wasn't calm myself.

Sara was still staring at the spot where the car

had been.

I moved around her. My feet felt as if they were glued to the ground. I had to drag them forward at every step.

"Stay there," I told Sara.

That was dumb, too. Sara wasn't moving at all.

I still don't know why I did the next thing I did. I stretched out my right hand, leaned forward a little, and began inching ahead to where the car had been.

"Daniel, be careful!" Sara whispered sharply behind me.

I kept inching forward.

"Daniel, don't!"

I inched forward a little more.

"Daniel, please!" Sara kept whispering behind me. Then, all of a sudden, my heart stopped beating.

My fingertips had touched something icy cold! I snatched my hand back and shivered.

I felt Sara clutching at my sweater.

I was still shivering from touching whatever it was. But there was something familiar about it.

Very slowly, I stretched my hand out again. The back of my neck tingled. My flesh crawled. I held my breath.

It was cold. It was hard. It was smooth.

Suddenly, I knew what it was.

"Sara," I said, "you're not going to believe this."

Behind me, Sara made some sound in her throat that wasn't even a word.

"It's the car," I said. "It's here. We just can't see it."

I reached out again. Right in front of me, in bright daylight, I saw my fingers stop moving when they touched something I could not see.

I slid my fingers a little to the side. Then I slid them up a little. Yes, no doubt about it. It was definitely the car. Now I could feel the door handle.

"You feel it, Sara," I said quietly.

I had to grab her arm and force her to move it forward.

It was pretty creepy standing there, touching something you could not see.

It took both of us a few minutes to get used to

the idea.

Slowly, with Sara staying right behind me, I moved forward. My hand slid along the side of the car.

I started with the left rear door handle. Then I got to the front door handle. Then, finally, I felt the rear view mirror.

"Sara," I whispered, "I want to go all the way around. Just to be sure."

"Do we have to?" she whispered back.

"Yes," I said. "Stay close to me."

I didn't have to tell her that twice.

Slowly, carefully, we edged around the front of the car. Then we moved back along the right side of it until I felt the front door handle.

"Okay," I said. "Here's our plan."

"We have a plan?" Sara said.

Not exactly, I said to myself. I still had to think it up.

I looked quickly all around.

The sun was shining brightly. In front of the cabin, a grassy slope went down to the road. Behind the cabin, there was a steeper but shorter slope that ended at the edge of some woods.

There was nobody in sight. That was a good thing. If anybody was watching us, they would have thought we had lost our minds completely.

Inside the cabin, I could hear Mom humming a song. I just hoped she would not come out to see what we were doing.

"Here's what we're going to do," I told Sara. "We still have to get those apples out of the car. Maybe then, the car will become visible again."

"Why?"

How was I supposed to answer that?

"Maybe the ghost will be finished having fun with us then," I said. "Besides, we have to stand up to the ghost. We have to show it we're not afraid."

Sara didn't say anything to that, but I couldn't blame her. We were both afraid and we both knew it.

"Anyway," I added, "can you think of a better plan?"

Sara shook her head.

"So let's get started," I said. "When I open the door, we'll just start grabbing the apples and throwing them back there."

I pointed to the slope at the back of the cabin.

"Just throw them that way, into the woods," I said. "And do it as fast as you can. Mom might come out at any second."

"Is the door unlocked?" Sara whispered.

I crossed my fingers and held them up in front of her.

"I hope so!" I said. "Are you ready?"

Sara nodded.

"Okay," I said. "Here goes."

I felt around in mid-air for the handle of the door. I put my fingers in the right position. Silently, I counted to myself. One. Two. Three.

I pulled on the door handle. The car door came open.

"Oof!" I said, as something slammed into my stomach and something else punched me in the chest.

Behind me, I heard Sara gasp.

I fell backwards and landed on top of her on the ground.

Something was kicking and punching me all over my body!

Chapter Fifteen

The apples!

It was the apples sliding and tumbling out of the car. That's what had knocked me down.

I was hoping that Mom and Dad did not hear the noise we were making.

"Sara, get up!" I whispered. "We have to get rid of these apples."

I scrambled to my feet. And as soon as I started moving around, I felt the apples. They were everywhere. They were all over the ground around us.

Sara looked terrified, but she was getting to her feet.

I knew she was trying to be brave, and I was proud of her.

Even if she was my little sister.

She bent over and started feeling the grass

around her feet.

"They're everywhere," she said. "There must be a million of them."

"Don't *count* them," I said. "Just get *rid* of them. Throw them or roll them down the hill to the woods. Do it quick!"

She was already starting.

"I'm going to open the back door now," I told her.

I felt around for the handle of the back door and pulled the door open.

Another ton of apples came thumping and banging out of the back of the car.

We must have really looked crazy out there. We were crawling around on our hands and knees and feeling all over the grass. And we were throwing invisible apples down into the woods.

If anyone had seen us, they would have locked us up.

When the ground right around us seemed to be getting clear of apples, I whispered to Sara again.

"I'm going to get in the car now. I have to pull all the rest of the apples out."

She nodded but kept working.

I had to feel my way into the invisible car. I also had to be careful not to step or kneel on any apples. I did not want to leave any crushed apples or sticky juice inside the car or on the seats.

There were still plenty of apples in there. As fast as I could, I swept them off the seat and onto the floor. Once they were on the floor, at least I knew that they were all together.

Then I crouched on the seat. Using my hands, I swept them off the floor, out the door, and onto the ground.

First I did the front of the car, then the back.

There must have been a zillion apples in that car!

I felt all around inside the car one more time, just to be sure. It's a good thing I did. I found three apples left on the dashboard.

I picked them up, slid out of the car, and tossed them down the hill.

Then I closed the two doors of the car.

Sara was still crawling around, feeling everywhere for apples. But now she wasn't finding any more of them.

I hoped we had gotten rid of all of them.

Then I nearly jumped out of my skin!

"What are you two doing?" a deep voice boomed at us.

I spun around and fell right on my behind. I had forgotten that I was crouching on the ground. Sara was about six feet away from me.

And my father was standing near the back of the car with his hands on his hips.

The look on his face showed only one thing. It showed that he thought his two children had gone completely nuts.

With all the worrying and working and thinking I'd been doing all day, I suddenly felt exhausted.

But I had to think fast again.

"It's a game, Dad," I said. "Just a dumb game we were making up."

Suddenly, Sara turned into a great actress.

"Oh, Dad," she said, "I guess we looked pretty silly, huh?"

"Well . . . " Dad said slowly. He started to smile.

"Besides," Sara said, "it's starting to get a little cooler, and we were moving around to keep warm."

I started hoping the little actress wouldn't say too much and give everything away.

"Well, okay," Dad said. "If you get cold, come inside and get your jackets."

"We will, Dad," I said as he turned back toward the front of the cabin. "Count on it."

Neither one of us moved until he had turned the corner of the cabin.

Then I looked at Sara.

She raised her hand and pointed at something behind me.

But this time she was grinning.

I turned my head, and now I saw it too.

The car!

It just stood there on the grass, right beside the cabin, shining in the sunlight as if nothing weird had ever happened.

I gave a big sigh of relief.

I was still sitting on the ground. Sara came over to me quickly on her knees.

She put her mouth near my ear.

"We won!" she whispered loudly. "We won! We got all the apples out of the car. And now the ghost knows we're not afraid of it anymore. So now it'll leave us alone!"

I wasn't too sure about that. But I certainly did feel better about things.

After all, we had beaten the ghost. It had given back the car.

Maybe now we were going to be able to enjoy this vacation after all.

"You did great, Sara," I said.

She didn't say anything, but I could see that she felt really good when I said that.

Then, all of a sudden, I felt even more miserable than I had before.

"Daniel. Sara."

It was Mom. She was standing near the front corner of the cabin.

"You two could do me a really big favor," she said, smiling. "I promised your father I'd make some baked apples, but the ones we have are McIntosh. They're the wrong kind. I need Rome apples for baking."

Oh, no! Please, no!

"Would you mind taking another ride to the cider mill and getting a bag of Rome apples?" Mom glanced at her watch. "You'll have to leave pretty soon, though, so you can be back while there's still daylight. I don't want you out in the dark."

You can bet I didn't want that, either.

"Sure, Mom," I said. I tried not to let my voice sound as weak as I felt.

"In fact, we'll go right away," I said. "We don't want to be riding our bikes on the road after dark."

"No, we sure don't," Sara said beside me, but now she was talking in that scared little voice again.

We got our jackets, and in about two minutes we were rolling down the hill toward the road.

I could not believe it.

For the second time that day, we were going back to the cider mill where all the trouble had started in the first place.

Chapter Sixteen

At the bottom of the hill, I stopped my bike to talk to Sara.

When she came up beside me, I tried very hard to look serious but confident. I figured that, if she was terrified, she might do something dumb — and then we would both be doomed.

But I wasn't just worried about what Sara might do. I was worried about myself. The truth is that I did not feel nearly as brave as I tried to pretend I was.

"Listen, Sara," I said. "We did a great job back there at the cabin. Just like you said, we showed the ghost that we're not afraid of it."

"We sure did!" Sara said. Thinking about it made her feel strong again.

"But," I said, "we can't act like we're safe."

Sara just stared at me. She knew what I was going to say.

"Because we're not," I said.

My words seemed to hang in the air like misty little bits of fog with no breeze to blow them away.

"What are we going to do?" Sara asked.

I did my best to make my voice sound strong.

"We're going to show the ghost we're not afraid. We're going to ride our bikes right up to the front door of the mill."

"We are?" Sara said.

"We are," I said. "And then you're going to stand right there by the door with the bikes."

"Where will you be?" Sara's voice was getting tinier with every word she said.

"I'll go inside and get the apples. If there aren't many people on line, it should just take a minute. Or half a minute."

Sara looked even more unhappy than she had before.

"A lot can happen in half a minute," she said.

"I know," I said. "We'll just have to be as quick as we can. I'll go in for the apples. I'll never be out of sight. And when we have the apples, we are outta there!"

By now, Sara was so unhappy that her chin was resting on her chest and she was staring at the ground.

I felt exactly the same way, but I had to pretend I felt brave.

"C'mon," I said. "Let's get going. The sooner we do it, the sooner it's over."

I glanced up at the sky.

"And we have to be quick and get home before dark."

That got Sara moving. In a second, she was on her bike and racing down the road.

I jumped on my bike and followed. I had to pedal hard to catch up, she was going so fast.

After a short distance, we had to slow down because the gravel road was so uneven and bumpy.

We didn't talk all the rest of the way. I let Sara get a little bit ahead of me so I could always see that she was safe.

I saw her looking all around as she rode, looking at the fields and the woods on either side of the road.

I was doing the same thing.

It seemed to be taking us an awfully long time to get to the cider mill.

Then, all of a sudden, I saw the mill up ahead.

"Wait!" I called to Sara.

We stopped side by side. Slowly and carefully, I looked at the road, the parking lot, the mill, the doorway to the store, the people going in and out. I was searching and searching for anything that looked wrong.

Everything looked perfectly right and normal.

"Okay, Sara," I said. "It looks safe."

We mounted our bikes to ride the short distance to the store entrance at the front of the mill.

We began rolling forward. Sara was a little ahead of me.

Suddenly, Sara's bike came to a complete stop, teetered over to one side, and Sara went crashing to the ground.

She didn't scream, but I heard a *whump!* sound as if all the air had been knocked out of her lungs.

I slid my bike to a halt, jumped off, and ran to where she was lying.

Her eyes were closed. She looked as if she had stopped breathing.

Chapter Seventeen

"Sara!" I cried. I shook her by the shoulders. "Sara! Sara! Wake up! Get up!"

Her eyelids fluttered weakly. Slowly, she opened her eyes and looked at me.

It looked as if it was hard for her to talk.

"Who . . . " she began. "Who are you?"

Her eyes closed.

She didn't even know me!

I shook her shoulders again.

Now she didn't even open her eyes.

What was I going to do?

A million thoughts zoomed through my brain.

What if Sara was dead?

What if some of the adults at the mill saw us, right there in the middle of the road? What could I possibly say that would make sense?

They would think I was crazy. They might even think that I was the one who killed her. Then Sara would be dead and I would be in prison for the rest of my life!

Chapter Eighteen

I shook Sara by the shoulders again.

She had to wake up!

"Ooooh!" she moaned.

Slowly her eyes began to open and she moved her head from side to side.

"Sara!" I cried.

"Ow! I hurt all over!" she said. Her voice shook with fear.

"My ankle hurts! And my knee! And my elbow! And my hand! Ow! And my head hurts, too!"

"You're alive!" I cried. That was the most important thing in the world to me at that moment.

"C'mon," I said. "First we have to get you out of the road."

"Ow!" Sara yelped again, when she tried to get up. "I don't think I can move."

"You have to!" I said quickly. "You catch your breath. I'll move the bikes."

I don't know how I did it. In about two seconds, I had moved both bikes off the road and hidden them in the ditch beside it. We were at the place where the apple orchard behind the mill came right up to the road, but I did not have time to think about that.

I raced back to Sara. She was struggling to her feet. She kept one hand up to the side of her head.

I helped her to the side of the road.

"What happened?" I asked her. "What happened? I need to know!"

Sara's voice was still shaky when she answered.

"I ran into something," she said. "Like a wall or a fence, maybe."

My head snapped around and I looked at the road where she had fallen.

There was nothing there. Nothing I could see!

Then a truly weird thing happened.

Just for a second — maybe even less than a second — a white wooden fence appeared, stretching right across the road.

And then, as quickly as it had appeared, it was gone. Completely gone!

I must have groaned or something, because Sara said, "What? What?"

That ghost was just laughing at us, mocking us with its power. But I couldn't say that to Sara.

"Nothing," I said, as calmly as I could. "I think I twisted my ankle too. It just hurt for a second, then."

"Oh," Sara said.

I don't think she believed me but I was sure she didn't really want to know what I was thinking.

"I have a new plan," I said suddenly.

Sara's face grew even more pale.

"What?" Sara asked. She was staring at me with her eyes wide open.

I was thinking as fast as I could.

"I know!" I said. "The ghost is waiting for us here. So we'll have to get to the mill by another way."

But Sara saw the flaw in my plan at once, just as I saw it myself.

"Daniel, the ghost could be anywhere!"

I had no answer for that because I knew Sara

was right.

"I know," I said, as calmly as I could. "We'll just have to take the risk."

"What risk?" she asked. "How are we going to get to the mill?"

I took a deep breath before I answered.

"Through the orchard," I said.

"Through the orchard?" Sara gasped. "Go through the orchard? Daniel, you must be out of your mind!"

Chapter Nineteen

I did not answer her for a few seconds.

And for those few seconds, I thought she might be right. Maybe I was going crazy with fear.

I fought to push away that thought.

"Just listen to me, Sara," I said. "Here's what we're going to do."

My mind was racing, trying to picture each step in my plan.

"We're going to leave the bikes here. Then we're going to sneak through the orchard. We'll go in right here."

I pointed to the nearest apple trees, which were only about twenty feet away from us. Sara turned her head to look, but she was too frightened to speak.

"We're going to sneak through the orchard,

but we're going fast. Sort of sneak-running," I said.

Sara just stared at me.

"Do you understand?" I asked her.

Sara only nodded her head. I had never seen her eyes look so big before.

"I know it's dangerous to go through the orchard," I said. "But something is blocking the road. So we can't go that way. We can't get to the front entrance that way."

Sara looked nervously at the orchard again. It was late afternoon now. The shadows of the apple trees were making the orchard darker by the second.

"So we'll go through the orchard to the back of the mill?" Sara asked.

"Right," I said. I was glad Sara was getting over her fear. That helped me get over my own.

Then I said, "Oh!" I had just thought of something else.

"The bikes," I said.

Moving quickly, I turned Sara's bike around and leaned it against the side of the ditch next to the road. Then I did the same with mine.

"There," I said. "Now, when we come back for

the bikes, they'll be facing the right way. We'll be able to make a quicker escape."

I turned back to Sara.

"Are you okay now?" I asked her. "Can you stand up?"

"I think so," she said.

Slowly and carefully, she stood up. She had to put her hand on my arm to steady herself.

"My ankle hurts," she said. "I must have twisted it when I fell."

"Can you walk?" I asked.

Sara took a couple of shaky steps.

"It hurts," she said. "But I think I can walk on it if we go slow."

"Sara," I said, "we can't go slow. We have to go as fast as we can."

"Maybe I better wait here," she said so quietly I could barely hear her.

"No!" I said firmly. "You can't wait here because I can't let you out of my sight. Something might happen to you."

"How far is it?" Sara asked.

"Not far," I said. "Look."

I pointed through the trees in the orchard. We had to go in a straight line through the trees, then across a short open space, around the edge of the pond, and then to the back of the mill.

"It just sounds like a long distance," I said. "Look! You can see the back of the mill from here."

Sara looked where I was pointing. After a few seconds, she said, "Okay."

"How's your ankle?" I asked her.

"Okay, I think," she said.

"Then let's go," I said. "Follow me. And stay close."

I took a deep breath, moved toward the nearest trees, and stepped into the shadows of the orchard.

I was ready to start running toward the mill. I reached back to take Sara's hand.

Bonk!

Something hit me on the head!

I grabbed for Sara's hand, got it, and started running.

Bonk! Bonk! Bonk!

Apples were falling on our heads from the trees. The ghost was bombing us with apples!

Chapter Twenty

I raced for the back of the mill. Nothing was going to stop me.

"Daniel! Daniel! My ankle! Ow!" Sara was gasping behind me.

I held her hand tighter and kept running.

The short distance seemed like a million miles, but at last we reached the back of the mill.

I slumped against the wall, out of breath. My head hurt from all the apples that had bounced off it.

Sara slid to the ground beside me.

"Ow, Daniel, my ankle really hurts now!" she said. "I can't walk on it anymore."

"We'll just rest here for a minute and catch our breath," I said. "Maybe your ankle will feel better then."

"Daniel, it won't!" Sara said. "It hurts too

much. I can't go any farther."

"You have to!" I said. "I can't leave you here!"

I didn't even see the man come up beside us. I jumped when I heard his voice.

"You kids okay?" he asked.

I'm getting careless, I thought. The man had just gotten off a tractor that was stopped right in front of us. Behind the tractor was a wagon filled with apples.

"Oh, we're okay," I said quickly. I tried to form my face into a smile. I'm not sure that I succeeded.

If I told him the truth, he would think we were both nuts.

"Yeah, we're fine," Sara said in her actress voice.

"Okay," the man said.

He opened both halves of a wide doorway in the back wall of the mill. Inside, I could see a bin that was filled halfway with apples. From the middle of the apples a conveyor belt sloped upward out of sight.

"Want to see how this works?" the man asked.

He grinned.

I did *not* want to see how it worked, but I didn't want the man to know how I felt.

"Sure," I said.

"Okay," he said, "just stay out of the way a second."

He got back up on the tractor and moved it until the wagon was right beside the wide doorway. Then he got off and opened a little door in the wall that revealed a small control panel.

"Watch!" he said.

He pushed a button on the control panel. The conveyor belt started moving, carrying apples from the bin up and up and up to where they disappeared someplace out of sight.

Then I heard the sound we had heard yesterday.

Globbeta-glotch! Globbeta-glotch! Globbeta-glotch!

It was the sound of the apples being crushed by the machinery.

"Wow! That's cool!" I said.

The man pushed the button again and the belt

stopped moving and the horrible crunching sounds grew silent.

The man went to the wagon and fiddled with something on the side of it. The side of the wagon tilted slowly upward and, with a sound like thunder, the whole load of apples went crashing into the bin.

"Wow!" I said again. I would have said anything just to make that man go away.

Finally, he was finished. He got back on the tractor and drove off.

"Okay," I said to Sara. "Let's get going. Now we just have to get the bag of apples for Mom. Then we race back to our bikes and get away from here!"

"I can't, Daniel," Sara said. "My ankle hurts too much. You go ahead. I'll be okay here."

"Sara, you can't stay here alone!"

"I have to," Sara said. "Maybe my ankle will be better by the time you come back."

I didn't like it but I didn't have any choice.

"Okay," I said. "But be sure you stay right here! Don't move an inch away from this spot."

"I won't," Sara said. "I promise."

"Okay," I said. "I'll go as fast as I can."

And I was off! I ran around the back of the mill, down along the side, past the stairs, and around the corner to the front.

I dashed into the store, pulling the money out of my jeans as I ran.

So far, so good. Nothing had attacked me.

I got the bag of apples and paid for it. I stuffed the change in my pocket.

In a second, I was racing back to where I had left Sara. I came speeding around the corner of the mill.

Sara was nowhere in sight. She was gone!

And from inside the mill I heard that horrible sound again.

Globbeta-glotch! Globbeta-glotch! Globbeta-glotch!

Chapter Twenty-One

"Sara!" I yelled. "Sara!"

Globbeta-glotch! Globbeta-glotch! Globbeta-glotch! That was all I could hear!

"Sara!" I yelled again. And then I thought I heard a faint voice calling my name.

"Sara! Where are you?"

Globbeta-glotch! Globbeta-glotch! Globbeta-glotch!

"Daniel!" That time I heard Sara's voice.

But where was she? I spun around, looking everywhere.

Globbeta-glotch! Globbeta-glotch! Globbeta-glotch!

"Daniel!"

She was inside the mill! My heart was pounding. The skin at the back of my neck was tingling.

"I'm coming, Sara!" I yelled.

My fingers tore at the latch on the double doors the man had opened before. It was stiff and tight. I had to pull hard on it, but at last it came loose.

I grabbed the handles on both doors and flung them open to the sides.

Inside, I saw the bin of apples. It was nearly full to the top. I saw the conveyor belt. It was moving up and up, carrying apples to the cruncher up above.

And there was Sara!

She was in the bin with the apples. At first I couldn't figure out what she was doing.

Then I saw. Her shirt was caught in the conveyor belt. Slowly, slowly, it was pulling her up and up toward the machinery that crushed the apples.

Globbeta-glotch! Globbeta-glotch! Globbeta-glotch!

In another couple of seconds, it was going to crush her!

Chapter Twenty-Two

I did not even stop to think what I was doing.

In a second, I climbed into the bin of apples and grabbed at Sara.

The conveyor belt was pulling her upward.

I was pulling her downward.

"Help me, Daniel!" Sara cried.

I was trying, but she just kept moving slowly upward.

I tried to reach around her to find where her shirt was caught in the belt. But I could not find it.

"Help!" she cried again.

Right above our heads, I heard that horrible sound.

Globbeta-glotch! Globbeta-glotch! Globbeta-glotch!

In a second, it was going to go *globbeta-glotch!* with Sara!

Chapter Twenty-Three

I didn't know what to do. I pulled and pulled but she was not coming free. And the belt just kept pulling her slowly up and up.

Then I had a last, desperate idea.

I jumped upward and caught hold of Sara's shoulders.

I grabbed her. I lifted my feet out of the apples in the bin and hung all my weight on her shoulders.

And in a second, the two of us fell with a crash into the bin of apples. Our combined weight had pulled her free.

"Get out!" I shouted. "Get out!"

Slipping and sliding among the apples, we scrambled to the side of the bin.

In another second, the two of us tumbled over the edge of the bin and landed in a heap on the ground.

"Come on!" I cried. "Let's get outta here!"

"Daniel, my ankle still hurts!" Sara gasped.

"I'll help you run," I said. "Lean on me."

Sara leaned on my shoulder and we moved as fast as we could toward the orchard. Sara was limping badly, but fear made us both keep going.

I was not happy about running that short distance through the orchard, where we had been bombarded with apples. But that seemed like nothing now, compared to what had happened to us since.

This time, nothing touched us. No apples fell from the trees. No ghosts tried to grab us.

We made it back to the bikes. They were right where we had left them.

"Daniel," Sara said quickly, her voice shaking. "My ankle hurts so much. I don't think I can ride my bike."

"You have to!" I said. "That's all there is to it. You have to!"

And then I thought of something and my heart went *thump!* in my chest.

The apples! I had forgotten the bag of apples

for Mom!

"Wait here!" I snapped at Sara.

Before I even had time to think about what I was doing, I began racing at top speed between the apple trees. I sped around the pond and across to the back of the mill.

I saw the bag of apples right where I had dropped it.

From inside the mill, I heard that awful sound.

Globbeta-glotch! Globbeta-glotch! Globbeta-glotch!

I grabbed the bag of apples.

"Come on, you ghost! I dare you to get us!" I said to the back of the mill. But I did not say it very loud. I think I was afraid the ghost might actually hear me.

Then I raced back around the pond, through the orchard, and back to where Sara waited with the bikes.

"Ride!" I yelled at her. "I don't care if your ankle hurts! Just get on your bike and ride!"

I dumped the apples into the basket on my handlebars. We pushed our bikes up onto the road.

We hopped on and raced away from there as fast as we could pedal.

We were halfway back to the cabin before we stopped to catch our breath.

"How's your ankle?" I asked Sara.

"It still hurts," she said. "But I can pedal with it."

Now I had to ask the really scary question.

"What happened back there while you were waiting for me?"

I almost didn't want to know the answer, because if Sara had been hurt, it would have been my fault. I should never have left her alone.

"Something grabbed me," Sara said. She shivered and hugged her elbows to her sides. "It just grabbed me and picked me up and threw me in with the apples. It was horrible! It almost killed me!"

She was right. And it would have been my fault. Like so many other things.

"I'm sorry I left you alone," I said. I didn't know what else to say.

After a second, Sara said, "It's okay. It wasn't your fault. I was the one who said I'd wait there."

Then we were both silent, thinking about what had almost happened.

Then I thought of something else.

"Hey!" I said. "Maybe we've beaten it now. It did everything in its power to get us, but we got away. It even tried to kill you, but we still escaped."

Sara's face grew a little brighter.

"Yeah," she said, "and nothing happened when we ran through the orchard back to the bikes."

"That's right," I said. "And nothing happened when I ran back for the bag of apples."

"Right," Sara said. "And nothing happened to our bikes."

"Yeah," I said, "and nothing has happened to us on the road."

We both looked all around at the farms and the fields. Everything looked peaceful and normal.

Could it be that we had won?

Could it be that the horror was over?

Chapter Twenty-Four

Mom must have asked us a hundred times, but neither of us would eat a baked apple that evening.

And we would not drink apple juice or eat a plain apple, either.

No, thank you!

After dinner, Dad said we were all going to go horseback-riding the next day.

"Great!" I said.

"Bob, let's go past the mill on the way," Mom said. "I'd like to stop for a few minutes. You can go up to the second floor, you know, and see how the whole thing works. You can see how the apples are crushed into cider and everything. Kids, you'd like to see that, wouldn't you?"

My throat closed tight. I could not speak.

I gulped.

Dad looked at me closely and smiled.

"You kids didn't see any ghosts over there, did you," he asked, chuckling.

"No, Dad," I managed to say.

"Well, maybe you'll see them another time," Dad said. "You know, it's only two weeks till Halloween. And we'll still be here then. And everybody knows that Halloween is when ghosts really start acting up!"

"Bob, you're just being silly," Mom said.

She turned to Sara and me.

"Now, are you two sure you don't want a baked apple? They're really good."

I couldn't even answer. Neither could Sara.

"Sara? Daniel?" Mom said. "What's wrong with you two? You know, you both look like you really *have* seen a ghost!"

Chapter Twenty-Five

I hardly slept a wink that night.

I just tossed and turned. Every time I started to doze off, I'd suddenly wake up again.

And I could hear Sara. I knew she was doing the same thing.

Finally, I couldn't keep quiet any longer.

"Sara," I whispered. "Are you awake?"

"Yes," her voice came out of the dark.

"Can't you sleep?"

"Not really," I heard her say. "My nose is stuffed up. I think I'm getting a cold. Maybe that's why I can't sleep."

Her voice *did* sound a little odd.

"Well." I said, "I can't sleep because of . . . you know."

I just let my voice drift away. I didn't really

want to admit that I'd been afraid. After all, here we were safe in our beds hours later. Nothing had hurt us at all.

"Daniel?" Sara said.

"What?"

It was a while before she answered. And when she did, she spoke very slowly.

"You know," she said, "I don't think there was ever anything to be afraid of at the mill."

"You don't?" I said.

And now that I thought about it, I was sort of getting to feel the same way myself.

"Really?" I asked.

"Yeah, really," Sara said. "Think about it. Nothing really bad happened, right?"

"Well, not really, but . . . "

"Okay, so there was some weird stuff," Sara said. "Some stuff that didn't seem right. But I think we might have just imagined a lot of it."

"Imagined it?" I said. I couldn't really understand what Sara meant. And the truth was that I didn't really know what I thought myself.

"Yeah." she said. "Maybe we imagined it. Like

dreaming or something."

"Dreaming?" I said. I could hear myself sounding stupider and stupider every time I opened my mouth.

"Right," Sara said. "I mean, Dad told us that dumb story about the kids getting caught in the mill's machinery, and I think that did it. It made us think *we* might get killed. And then we thought every little thing that happened was being done by a ghost."

I thought about that. Something about what Sara was saying just didn't sound right to me, but I couldn't figure out what it was.

"Well, maybe," I said. I was going to have to think all this through again.

"You know, Daniel," Sara said, "I *do* think we imagined the whole thing."

Suddenly, I thought of something.

"What about the apples in the car?" I said. "Did we imagine *them*?"

"Did you *see* apples?" Sara asked.

"See them?" I asked. "Well, no. Not while we were getting them out of the car, anyway. But we both saw . . ."

"Did you *see* them?" Sara insisted. "I know we emptied them out of the car, but did you actually *see* them in your hands?"

She could sound very smart when she wanted to.

"I guess not," I said.

"Did Dad see any apples in the car?" she asked. When Sara wanted to make a point or win an argument, there was no stopping her.

"No," I said. I had the feeling I always have when I know I'm going to lose an argument, no matter what I say.

There was silence in the darkness. I knew that Sara was giving me time to see the only possible explanation.

She was the first to break the silence.

"I *told* you we imagined it," she said.

I was still trying to figure out something, but at that moment I didn't even know what it was.

"You know what I think?" Sara said suddenly.

I groaned inside. I'd heard that tone of voice before.

"No, what?" I said.

Whatever it was, I was pretty sure I wasn't going to like it.

"I think we should go back to the mill," Sara announced.

"Go back?" I said. I sounded like a stupid echo in the darkness. But I couldn't help it.

"Yes," she said.

"*Go back*?" I could hardly believe what she was saying.

"Yes," she said again. "And lower your voice or Mom and Dad will hear us."

"Sara . . . " I started to say.

"Come on," Sara said. "Let's go."

"What do you mean?" I said. "What are you talking about?"

"We're going back to the mill. Right now. So get moving."

I heard her feet hit the floor lightly.

"Sara!"

"Come on!" I could hear her moving across the room in the darkness.

"Come on!" she whispered again.

And she was gone.

I rolled out of bed. The floor felt cold beneath my feet.

I groped around in the darkness for my jeans.

And all I could think, over and over again, was: This is going to get us killed, for sure!

Chapter Twenty-Six

I caught up to Sara where we'd left our bikes at the rear of the cabin. She had hers turned around, ready to hop on and roll down the hill to the road.

"Sara!" I said.

"Lower your voice!" she whispered.

"Sara, we have to talk about this. You're acting like you're crazy or something."

"I'm not crazy."

"Sara, it's the middle of the night! It's dark out, haven't you noticed?"

"So," she said, in that superior tone of voice, "you're not afraid of the dark are you?"

"No, but . . . "

"So, c'mon, then," she said.

She hopped onto her bike. In another second, she was heading down the hill.

I thought she was nuts. Bonkers! Crazy!

But I had no choice. I got on my bike and followed her down the hill.

There was just enough moonlight for me to see her.

I tried to catch up. I had to talk to her.

I saw her reach the road and turn right, in the direction of the mill.

"Sara!" I called after her, softly, because I didn't want to be shouting in the silence.

She didn't hear me. Or she was ignoring me.

As soon as I turned onto the road, I pedaled as fast as I could.

I could see Sara ahead of me but I couldn't close the gap between us. I had to pedal as fast as I could just to keep her in sight.

What was wrong with her? What did she intend to do? What did she think she was going to prove?

I didn't call out to her again. I needed all of my breath just to pedal that bike and not let her get away.

Chapter Twenty-Seven

The moon was bright above my head as I raced down the road after Sara. I could just make out the surface of the road. I tried to steer around any shadows that might conceal potholes or ruts.

But I couldn't keep my eyes on the road every second. I had to watch Sara, too. She was moving so fast that I thought she'd get away from me.

The moonlight was bright enough to throw blurred shadows of trees across the road. The whole scene was creepy and scary, but I just kept pedaling.

What was wrong with Sara?

I was weakening. The muscles in my legs were burning from pumping the pedals so hard. I started to think I might have to stop when I saw Sara slow down ahead of me.

I'd been riding so hard and worrying so much

about Sara that I'd hardly noticed where we were. Now I could see. We had ridden all the way to the mill.

Ahead of me, Sara stopped her bike.

Just ahead on my left, I could see the apple orchard. And just past the orchard, I could see the dark, shadowy shape of the mill itself.

As I braked to a stop, Sara was already rolling her bike down into the ditch beside the road, exactly where we'd left the bikes before.

I was out of breath, but I managed to say, "Sara, what's wrong with you? What do you think you're doing?"

I sat on my bike for a few seconds, trying to catch my breath.

"Put your bike down here with mine," Sara said.

I noticed that she didn't sound out of breath at all.

I rolled my bike off the road and into the ditch. Then I stood up and put my hands on my hips.

"Sara!" I said firmly. "Just stand here a minute. Tell me what's going on? *What do you think you're doing?*"

Sara stared at me for several seconds before answering.

Even in the moonlight, I could see that hard look she always got on her face when she intended to get her own way,

And her eyes looked dark and hollow, too, but maybe it was only because of the moonlight and the shadows.

"Daniel," she said finally. "Don't you understand?"

"Understand *what?*"

I did not understand what was going on. I did not understand Sara. And I did not understand what I was doing out here in a ditch beside this deserted road in the darkness, and almost within apple-throwing distance of the mill.

In fact, there was only one thing I was sure of. I was sure that it was a mistake for us to be here.

Probably a fatal mistake.

If we'd been in danger in broad daylight, what horrible things could happen to us out here in the middle of the night?

I was sweating from riding the bike. A cool breeze touched the back of my neck and made me shiver.

All around, it seemed like there was nothing but emptiness. Nothing but silence and a chilly breeze. Nothing but silvery moonlight and the dark shadows of trees that slid across the ground.

I shivered again.

I could just make out Sara's face in the moonlight, but I couldn't see her eyes.

I took hold of her arm.

"Sara!" I said. "Sara, will you tell me what you're doing? Because, as far as I can see, you've gone totally nuts!"

"No way," she said. "No, Daniel. That's not it. That's not what's happening."

"Then what *is* happening?"

"Come with me," she said.

I thought I must be going nuts myself. Sara's voice sounded different again. It sounded sad and lonely, sort of, and soft, and far away.

"Come with me," she said again. "I'll show you something."

"Where?"

"Just come with me, Daniel."

"Tell me where!" I demanded.

Sara shook her elbow free of my grip.

But then she reached out and took my hand.

And then the weirdest and creepiest and scariest thing of all happened. Worse even than everything that happened to us before.

When Sara's hand touched mine, it felt cold and clammy, like a fish, maybe, or like the skin of something that lived under rocks and never came out in the daylight.

My flesh crawled. I had goose bumps up and down my arms and on my neck. I shivered so hard and so suddenly that my teeth chattered.

"Sa . . ." I was shivering so much that I couldn't even say her name.

"Daniel," Sara said, "just come with me."

Her voice was soft and whispery, like the sound of a breeze blowing through the trees.

Her hand tightened on mine. Her skin still felt cold and damp.

"Just come with me," she said again, so softly I

could hardly hear her. Or maybe she said nothing and I just imagined that I heard something like a human voice.

I was going crazy. Or something even worse.

Sara tugged gently with that cold hand on my own.

She moved slowly, still holding my hand. We stepped into the deep, dark shadows of the orchard.

Chapter Twenty-Eight

The trees whispered to me.

Above my head, the branches of the trees swayed and moved, touched each other and made a sighing sound. It was a strange sound, one I'd never heard before.

Yet, at the same time, it sounded familiar. It had no words. It made no sense. But somehow it made me think I should be able to understand it.

I had the feeling that, any second now, the sound in the trees would speak to me and tell me something horrible and terrifying.

How big was this orchard?

It seemed to take forever to cross the orchard toward the mill. We walked and walked, Sara still holding my hand, and we didn't even seem to be half-way across yet.

The more we walked, the deeper and darker the shadows grew.

"Don't be afraid, Daniel."

It was Sara's voice. And it was *not* Sara's voice.

Maybe it was the voice of the breeze. Maybe it was the voice of the apple trees. Maybe it was the voice of the night.

"It's all right, Daniel," Sara said.

Or maybe the night whispered the words in my ear.

"Everything is going to be all right. Very soon now. Yes. Very soon, everything will be all right."

Sara's grip on my arm drew me further into the orchard, into the darkness.

It got darker and darker all around, I stretched my free hand out in front of me.

My fingers touched a face!

I knew it was a face, Sara's face, but it felt so cold and damp, like her hand!

I gasped.

"It's all right, Daniel," I heard Sara say in the voice that was not really hers. "Open your eyes."

I didn't even know my eyes were closed.

I opened them. It was night. Sara was beside me, her face hidden in the darkness. Behind her was the mill. I could just make out the doors of the big apple bin we had climbed inside before.

Suddenly, my mind felt like it was being torn apart, pulled in two different directions by forces much stronger than me.

One of those forces made me want to protect Sara. I wanted to get her away from this mill, away from the place where she'd nearly been killed.

The other force made me want to stay where I was. It made me feel that I belonged here.

I wanted so much to see Sara's face, but I couldn't. She kept it turned away from me.

I took a step closer. Still I could not make out her face in the darkness.

"Listen to me, Daniel," I heard her say in that whispery voice. "We're going to look inside."

Chapter Twenty-Nine

Sara let go of my hand. I could just see her shadowy form reaching out toward the rear wall of the mill. Then I heard metal scrape on metal.

My mind began to clear a little — at least enough for me to realize that this was the last place in the world I wanted to be.

"Daniel, help me with this," Sara said.

I thought her voice sounded more normal.

Or was I imagining that, too?

Sara struggled with the latches that held the doors closed.

My mind kept clearing, little by little, second by second.

Now — Yes! I was right!— I knew exactly where we were. Inside these doors was the apple bin, the place where Sara had nearly been caught in the conveyor belt and chewed up in the machinery of the mill.

"Sara!" I cried out.

For a second, I was amazed to find that I could talk again.

"Sara, we can't go in here again!"

"Yes, Daniel, we can," she said.

Her voice sounded more normal again, more the way it usually did. But now I noticed how calm she sounded. She didn't sound nervous or frightened at all.

"It's just the apple bin," I pleaded. "We've seen it already."

She ignored me.

"Swing that door back," she said.

We were doomed. I knew it, but something inside me made me obey her.

I swung my door back as she pulled at hers and swung it back, too.

Inside, the apple bin was a huge black rectangle of darkness.

Out of the corner of my eye, I saw Sara move. Immediately, I knew exactly what she was reaching for.

The click of the light switch sounded like a gunshot in the silence of the night.

Blinding yellow light flashed out from the apple bin.

I threw my arm up to protect my eyes. I took a couple of steps backward.

Still squinting, I saw that Sara had not moved.

For the first time since we'd gotten up, I got a good look at her face.

She looked . . . normal. And *that* suddenly seemed weird and terrible.

She took hold of my arm and gently pulled me forward, closer to the bin.

I looked inside.

I saw the bin. I saw the apples. I saw the conveyor belt, its bottom buried beneath the apples.

I looked at Sara.

"Look," she said softly, and pointed up. I looked where she was pointing, toward the top of the conveyor belt, where it passed through the ceiling into the floor above.

Instantly, I knew what I was looking at.

And I started to gag and choke.

Chapter Thirty

Blood!

There was blood everywhere!

The conveyor belt was red with bright, sticky blood.

Even the apples at the bottom of the conveyor belt were painted red with blood.

My stomach flip-flopped in my belly.

I did not want to see the rest of this, but I couldn't tear my eyes away from the sight.

At the top of the conveyor belt, where it passed through the ceiling, a bunch of bloody rags hung down. The rags were stuffed tightly into the opening.

There was even blood on the ceiling.

My knees felt like jelly. I put a trembling hand against the frame of the door to steady myself.

I had to wait a little longer for my stomach to settle.

I looked up again and struggled to stay calm.

There was no mistaking what I was looking at.

The bloody rags were blue jeans. Sara's jeans. And mine.

I forced myself to look more carefully.

I saw the blood-covered sneakers on our feet.

I saw a bit of Sara's yellow T-shirt that wasn't covered with blood. And I saw a little bit of my own orange-colored shirt. They were crumpled in the opening of the ceiling.

Where the bodies— *our* bodies— had been caught in the machinery, forced upward into the opening, and crushed.

I could not take my eyes away from that horrible sight.

I don't know how I formed words.

"Sara," I breathed, "how did you know?"

"During the night," she said quietly. "When I was trying to sleep. I didn't feel right. One second I just felt regular, but a little weird. And the next second, I just knew."

Silence.

I realized my mouth was still open. I closed it.

And slowly, very slowly, I began to get used to the idea.

I found I could look at the bodies up there without shivering or gagging. I could examine the way the clothing on them had been pulled or torn by the machinery.

It must have pulled and torn at the flesh — my flesh, Sara's flesh— in exactly the same way. Biting. Crushing. Tearing.

As I thought about it, it became interesting.

Our heads and arms must have been chewed up first. But they weren't thick enough to jam the machinery. The belt kept pushing us up and the machinery kept chewing at us.

From the way things looked up there, it must have been our hips that finally brought the machine to a stop.

And there we were.

"Well," Sara said. "Thanks anyway for trying to save me."

"Sure," I said. I chuckled a little. "Always glad

to help out."

Sara laughed.

"Always glad to lend a hand!" I said.

We laughed even harder.

Sara caught her breath. She tried twice to say something, but she kept on laughing,

Finally, she was able to get out the words she was trying to say.

"Thanks for sticking your nose into my business!"

We laughed and laughed.

"Thanks for . . . " Sara said, still laughing. "Thanks for . . . keeping an eye on me!"

We were doubled over with laughter.

It was a long time before we could catch our breath.

When we stopped laughing at last, I thought of something.

"Hey, we better put out the light and close those doors."

"Yeah," Sara said. "We don't want to spoil anybody's surprise in the morning."

That set us off laughing again, but we switched

off the light and latched the doors.

It was still the dark of night but I realized that now I could see just as well in darkness as in daylight.

We strolled away from the mill and sat on the same bench near the pond where we'd sat before, when the strange things first started happening.

"So what do you think we should do now?" Sara asked.

"Well," I said, "first we'll wait around to see the fun when somebody comes to open up in the morning."

"Yeah," Sara said. "That'll be great!"

"Then I think we'll just hang out for a while. Sooner or later, a couple of kids just like us are going to come along."

"Yeah," Sara said.

"Yeah." I said. "And then we'll start having some *real* fun!"

BE SURE TO READ THESE OTHER COLD, CLAMMY SHIVERS BOOKS.

THE ENCHANTED ATTIC

WHEN NICOLE AND HER LITTLE SISTER CASEY MOVE WITH THEIR FAMILY INTO AN OLD HOUSE IN MASSACHUSETTS, NICOLE THINKS THE NOISES SHE HEARS AT NIGHT ARE NOTHING MORE THAN THE SCURRYING OF MICE. BUT WHEN SHE STARTS TO HEAR EERIE MUSIC COMING FROM ABOVE HER CEILING, SHE REALIZES WITH A SHIVER THAT THE HOUSE MUST BE INHABITED BY SOMETHING FAR MORE TERRIFYING THAN MICE. AND IT IS UP TO HER TO FIND OUT WHAT IT IS.